fetch

Jorey Hurley

A Paula Wiseman Book
Simon & Schuster Books for Young Readers
New York London Toronto Sydney New Delhi

search

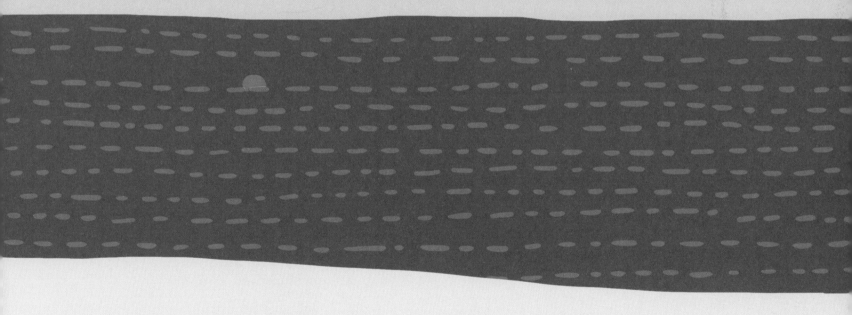

splash

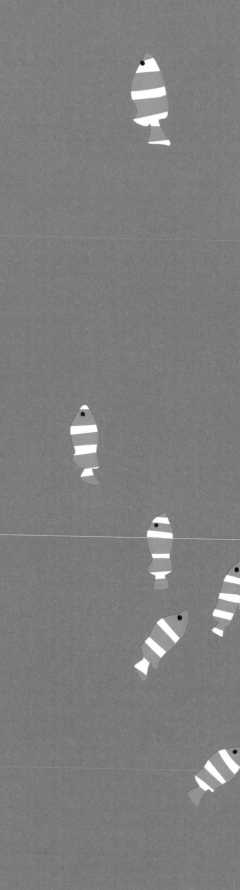

swim

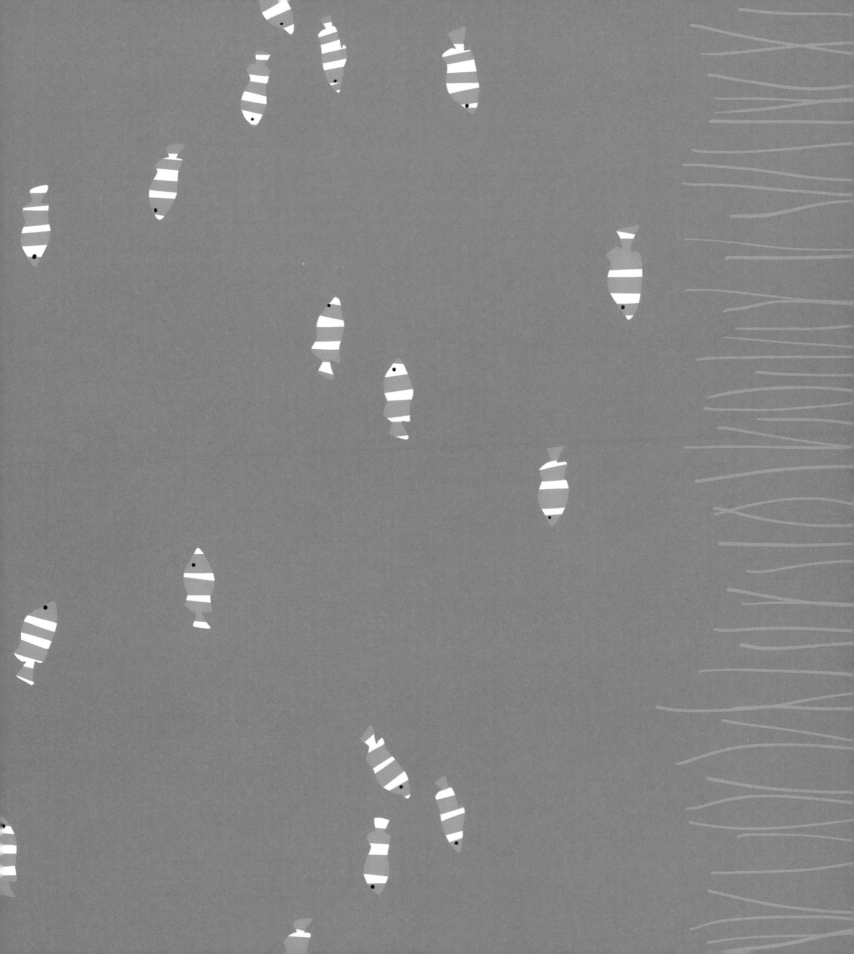

dive

seek

crash

shake

meet

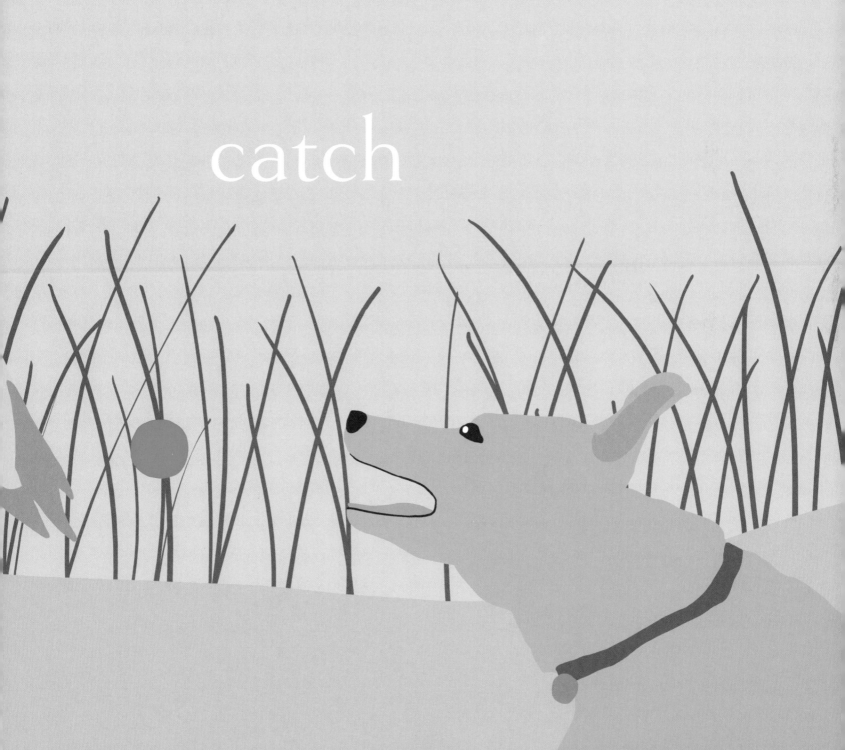

catch

run

play

float

find

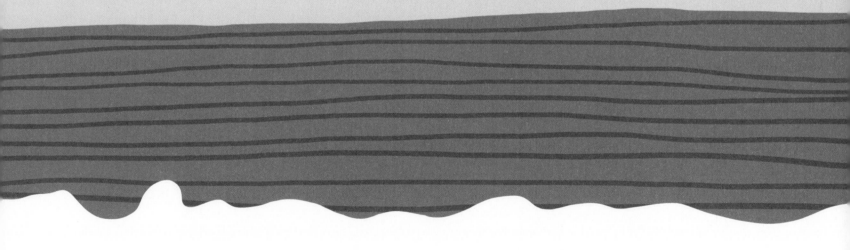

give

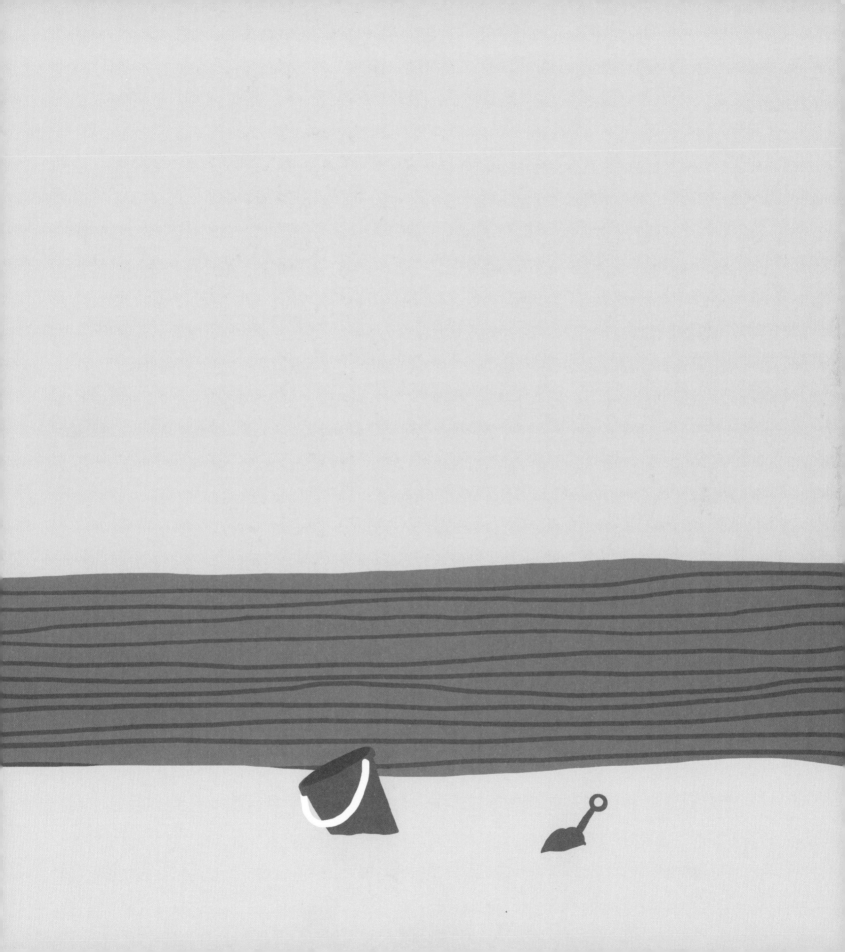

again?

for biscuit,
who rarely brings
back the ball

 SIMON & SCHUSTER BOOKS FOR YOUNG READERS • An imprint of Simon & Schuster Children's Publishing Division • 1230 Avenue of the Americas, New York, New York 10020 • Copyright © 2015 by Jorey Hurley • All rights reserved, including the right of reproduction in whole or in part in any form. • SIMON & SCHUSTER BOOKS FOR YOUNG READERS is a trademark of Simon & Schuster, Inc. • For information about special discounts for bulk purchases, please contact Simon & Schuster Special Sales at 1-866-506-1949 or business@simonandschuster.com. • The Simon & Schuster Speakers Bureau can bring authors to your live event. For more information or to book an event, contact the Simon & Schuster Speakers Bureau at 1-866-248-3049 or visit our website at www.simonspeakers.com. • Book design by Lizzy Bromley • The text for this book is set in Goldenbook. • The illustrations for this book are rendered in Photoshop. • Manufactured in China • 1114 SCP • 10 9 8 7 6 5 4 3 2 1 • Library of Congress Cataloging-in-Publication Data • Hurley, Jorey. • Fetch / Jorey Hurley. • pages cm • Summary: Illustrations and simple text follow a dog as it chases a ball at the beach. • ISBN 978-1-4424-8969-1 (hardcover) — ISBN 978-1-4424-8970-7 (ebook) [1. Dogs—Fiction. 2. Beaches—Fiction.] 1. Title. • PZ7.H956632Fet 2015 • E]—dc23 • 2014009875 [First edition]

author's note

We have a big, loud, mostly boxer mutt named Biscuit. Sometimes we take her to the dog beach near our home, where she spends her time finding smelly things to roll in and growling at other dogs who come near our beach blanket. While she's busy with that, we have a chance to watch the retrievers diligently charging through the surf to bring back their beloved soggy tennis balls. This book was inspired by the particularly tireless ball-retrieval efforts of one dog we often see: How far would she go? What's it like for her out there in the water?

This dog's journey, though fantastical, takes her past many of the creatures and plants she might encounter in the water just off the west coast of North America. First she swims over a sea grass meadow and a group of rockfish, common along the California coast. A little farther out she ventures underwater to investigate a harbor seal swimming through a forest of bull kelp, likely hunting for the small fish that thrive in kelp forests. After washing onto a new beach, our dog encounters a coastal animal very familiar to humans: the seagull. Like many inquisitive gulls, this group is investigating the dog's ball. Is it good to eat? Fortunately for the dog, it's not. With her ball secure in her mouth, she leaps into the water to head for home. On the way back she encounters some dolphins in deep water. Of all the sea creatures in this story, dolphins have the widest range, living in all parts of the world's oceans other than near the North and South Poles. As she gets closer to her home beach, our dog swims over a kelp forest where a midsize shark is hunting near the seafloor. This shark, like sharks in general, is busy hunting for her usual food and is not a threat to the dog. At last the dog charges onto her own beach. But with her mission accomplished, she's ready to head out again!

Jonas Hurley